PIR V PIR

THE *TERRIFIC TALE* OF A

WRITTEN BY **Mary Quattlebaum**

ILLUSTRATED BY **Alexandra Boiger**

ATE
S.
ATE

BIG, BLUSTERY MARITIME MATCH

Disney • HYPERION BOOKS
NEW YORK

Disney · Hyperion Books, 114 Fifth Avenue, New York, New York 10011-5690.
Printed in Singapore · First Edition · 1 3 5 7 9 10 8 6 4 2
F850-6835-5-10258 · This book is set in CC Treasure Trove. · Designed by Elizabeth H. Clark
Reinforced binding · Library of Congress Cataloging-in-Publication Data on file.
ISBN 978-1-4231-2201-2 · Visit www.hyperionbooksforchildren.com

To Christopher, a true treasure of a guy.
Here be the pirate tale ye craved.

~M.Q.

To Andrea, the Italian pirate in my life

~A.B.

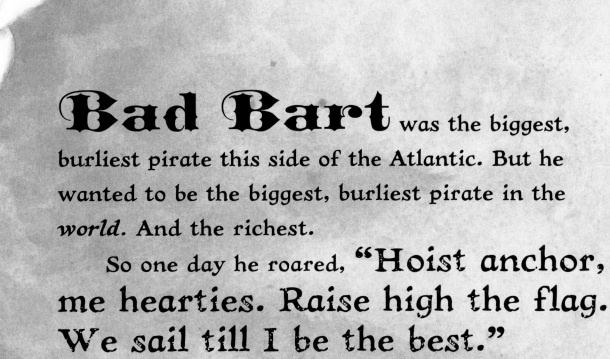

Bad Bart was the biggest, burliest pirate this side of the Atlantic. But he wanted to be the biggest, burliest pirate in the *world*. And the richest.

So one day he roared, "Hoist anchor, me hearties. Raise high the flag. We sail till I be the best."

Meanwhile, another pirate tapped her gold tooth and squinted out to sea.

Mean Mo was the maddest, mightiest pirate this side of the Pacific.

But am I the maddest, mightiest pirate in the *world*? she wondered. And the richest? So she set sail to find out.

The earth being round, the two met in the middle.

"Ahoy and avast!" roared Bad Bart. "Swing aside and let me pass."

"Swing yerself, ye scurvy dog!" Mean Mo roared right back.

Bad Bart blinked. He wasn't used to back talk.

He tried again:
"I be the biggest,
burliest—"

"And I be the
maddest, mightiest,"
Mean Mo interrupted. "I'll not
move for a rogue like ye."

"Rogue, am I?" Bad Bart
spat. "Deck swabber."

"Grog swiller."

"Landlubber."

"Bilge rat."

"Sea skunk."

"Gentleman,"
Mean Mo sneered.

"Lady."

Such insults! Bad Bart stomped off to his quarters, Mean Mo to hers. They sulked and stewed for two whole days before they came out again.

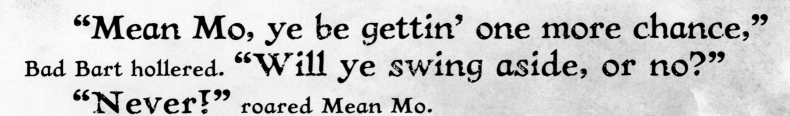

"Mean Mo, ye be gettin' one more chance," Bad Bart hollered. "Will ye swing aside, or no?"
"Never!" roared Mean Mo.
"Ready the cannons, men!"

"Wait a minute, Cap'n," piped up Bad Bart's rowdy crew. "Blowin' holes in the ships won't do."

Mean Mo's rascally crew agreed. "Ye need to figure this out fair and square, just the two of ye."

"A race!" Mean Mo challenged. "Unless ye be scared of a few wee sharks."

"Bring on the sharks!" Bad Bart roared. "At least their teeth be straighter than yours."

And with that, the two jumped into the sea.

They splashed and swam,

floated and **freestyled,**

dived and **dog-**paddled.

They wore out twenty sharks.
And at the end of three whole days . . . ?

Both crews agreed.

"I call for another contest." Bad Bart puffed out his chest. "Can that girly arm throw a cannonball?"

In answer, Mean Mo grabbed one and hurled it . . .
far out to sea.

Bad Bart grabbed and hurled.

This went on for four whole days,
till they ran out of cannonballs.

Then there was mast climbin'.

Arm wrestlin'.

And even hardtack eatin'.

Tie!

Well, Bad Bart may have been the biggest, burliest pirate, but, clearly, Mean Mo was the maddest and mightiest. 'Twas only one contest left.

It was time for a treasure count.
The crews poured out grog and
settled on deck.
Bad Bart dragged up his
treasure chest.
Mean Mo cracked her lock.

Such shine and sheen, such glitter and gleam.

Piles of gold and jewels, mounds of rings and belts and crowns.

Finally, Bad Bart leaned back and gasped, "1,953."

"1,953?" Mean Mo shrieked. "That means you—"

"—are the richest?" Bad Bart grinned.
"—are tied with me!" yelled Mean Mo. "I have 1,953 treasures, too."

Bad Bart stared at Mean Mo. He took in her mean green eyes and gold tooth. He thought of her mad hair and mighty muscles. Why, that lass could outswim sharks. She could heave cannonballs as big as his fist.

He fished a tiara from the top of his pile. **"Uh, hum,"** he muttered shyly. **"This be a little gift."**

Mean Mo stared at Bad Bart. She took in his bad black beard and crooked nose. She thought of his big chest and burly arms. Why, that man could climb masts and gobble hardtack like no one she'd ever seen (except herself).

Mean Mo grabbed a jeweled belt. **"Er."** She dug her toe into the deck. **"This be a present from me."**

Such a frenzy of sharing! Bad Bart and Mean Mo flung gems and coins and pins and crowns and rings till, when the air cleared . . .

. . . each had all the piles and mounds and treasures of the other.

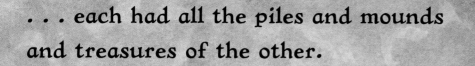

Tie!

"**Why, Bad Bart.**" Mean Mo threw back her head and laughed. "**Ye be a jewel of a man.**"

Bad Bart swept her a gallant bow. "**And ye be brighter than gold, me beauty.**"

Well, there was naught to do but tie
the knot. Bad Bart and Mean Mo roared,

"I do!"

so loud that they shook all the sharks.

Their crews threw hardtack and sang
sea chanteys and sent that bride and groom
off in fine style.

They honeymooned at the Blue Lagoon.

And now, me hearties, when ye sail the seven seas, be on the lookout for Bad Bart *and* Mean Mo. They be the biggest, maddest, mightiest, burliest couple this side of the Atlantic *and* the Pacific.

Listen close. Hear the sweet sayin's they croon?

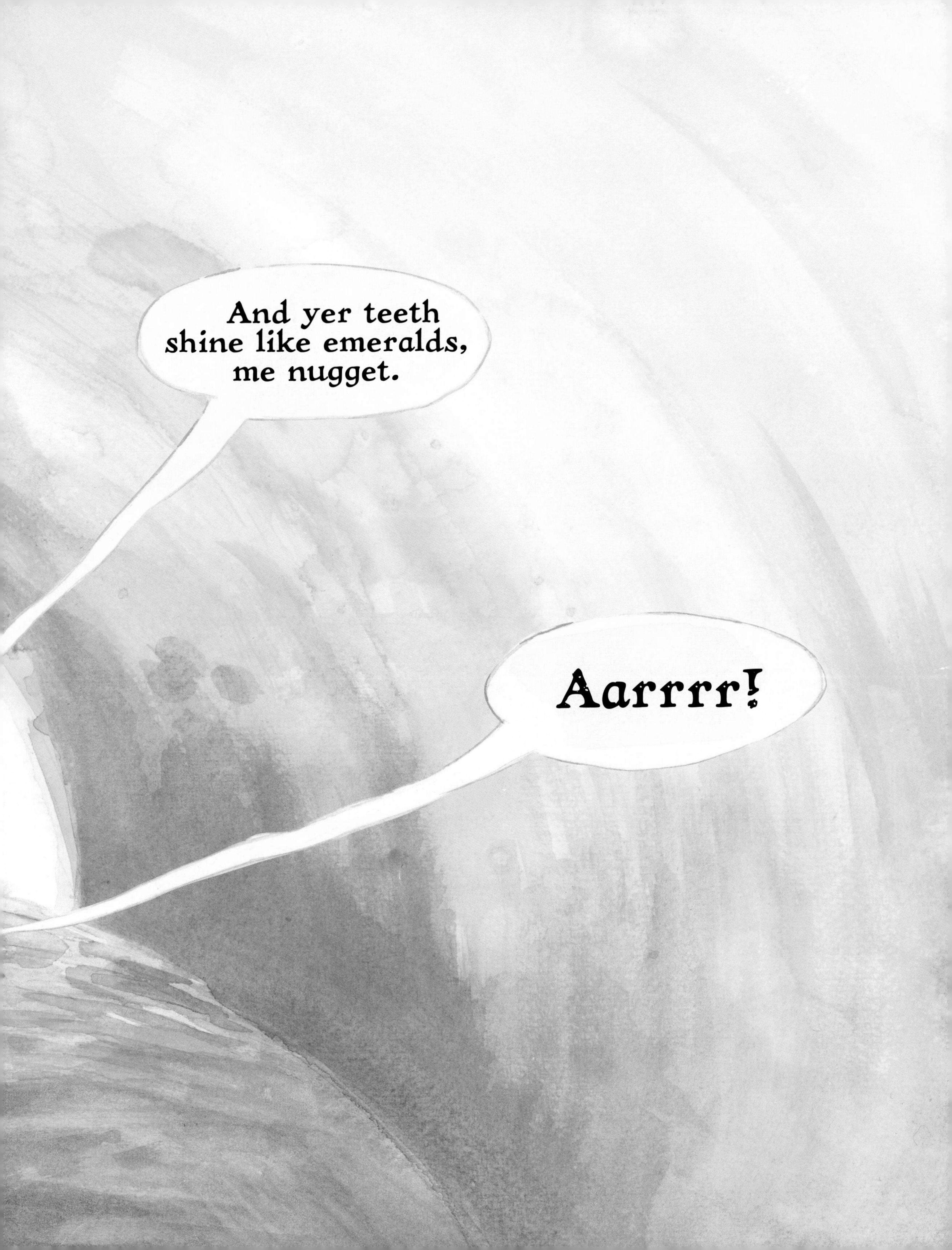
And yer teeth shine like emeralds, me nugget.
Aarrrr!